Ernest Myers

The Judgment of Prometheus

And other Poems

Ernest Myers

The Judgment of Prometheus
And other Poems

ISBN/EAN: 9783744782227

Printed in Europe, USA, Canada, Australia, Japan

Cover: Foto ©Andreas Hilbeck / pixelio.de

More available books at **www.hansebooks.com**

THE

JUDGMENT OF PROMETHEUS

AND OTHER POEMS

Oxford

PRINTED BY HORACE HART, PRINTER TO THE UNIVERSITY

THE

UDGMENT OF PROMETHEUS

And Other Poems

BY

ERNEST MYERS

London

MACMILLAN AND ·CO.

1886

DEDICATED BY THE AUTHOR

TO HIS WIFE.

che tra bella e buona
Non so qual sia più.

CONTENTS.

—◆—

THE 'Ode on the Death of General Gordon' and the poem entitled ' Rhodes' are reprinted from the *Fortnightly Review*, by the courteous permission of its publishers.

ERRATUM.

Page 6, line 3, *for* asken *read* ashen

[Myers' *Judgment of Prometheus*.]

THE JUDGMENT OF PROMETHEUS.

Strife having arisen between Zeus and Poseidon for the sake of Thetis, daughter of Nereus the sea-god, Prometheus was delivered from bondage on Caucasus and called to declare the award of Fate, known to him alone.

NOW through the royal hall, for Heaven's dread
 Lord
Wrought by the Fireking's hand, the assembled
 Gods,
Upon the morn appointed, thronging ranged
Expectant; mute they moved, and took their thrones,
Gloom on their brows, though Gods; so dark the
 dread
Of huge impending battle held their hearts,
Battle of brother Kings, Heaven and the Sea

In duel dire, convulsive war of worlds.

   So mused they all, and highest throned the
       Sire,

Lord of the lightning; on one side his Queen,

On the other, not less nigh, his chosen child

Pallas, most dear of all his race divine.

Somewhat aloof, yet in the upper hall,

The King Poseidon sate, and round his throne

Ocean, and all great Rivers of the world,

And all Sea-powers, and hoary Nereus nigh,

Nereus the ancient prophet, Thetis' sire.

Full many dooms he knew of days to be,

Yet fate of his own child no whit foresaw

More than the rest, and with the rest must wait

Sore wondering: she in a cool cave the while,

Her maiden chamber, far beneath the foam,

Trembling abode, till Iris flashing down

Should stand on the sea-cliff, and with clear voice

Hail her betrothed, and call her forth to hear

The dread assignment of her destined lord.

Silent the Gods sate all, but now the sound

They caught of coming steps, and from the door

Hermes drew nigh, and at his side a Form

August, of godlike presence, paced the hall.

Like to those heavenly Gods yet diverse he.

Not quite akin he seemed nor alien quite,

Of elder race than they, no seed of Zeus,

Earthborn although divine, and conqueror crowned

From wrestling long with pain, to other Gods

Rare visitant. On his immortal brow,

Ploughed by strange pangs, anguish unknown in

    Heaven,

Dwelt weightier thought than theirs, more arduous

    love.

With one accord the congregated Gods

In sudden homage from their golden thrones
Rose up for reverent greeting, as he came.
Then, as he gained their midst, the Thunderer
    spake :

" Hail, wondrous Titan, Earth's mysterious son,
Prophet Prometheus ! In this hour of need
Welcome thou art returned among the Gods,
Thyself a God : assume thy place, sit there
Acknowledged arbiter : what present doubt
Distracts our race divine thou knowest well
Already, and already know'st no less
The doom revealed that must that doubt dissolve.
Judge then, for all the Powers of Heaven are here
Expectant, and await thy final word."

He said, and all the assembly, when he ceased,
Murmuring well-pleased assent, had turned their
    gaze

There where the Titan sate, deep-plunged in
  thought;

Yet not for long; scarce had the murmur sunk

To silence, when his answering voice was heard:

  " Gods, and ye Kings of Heaven and of the Sea,

Who here demand my doom oracular,

That word of Fate ye seek, I bid you hear.

Not unto you, world-ruling Thrones divine,

Hath Fate this bride awarded whom ye woo.

Downward, far downward, bend your search, O
  Gods,

To once-despisèd earth, where lies a land,

Iolcus named, nigh to Olympus' foot,

There seek the sea-maid's lord by Fate assigned—

A man, and born of woman, but his blood

From thy celestial ichor, Sire of Gods,

Nathless derives; nor yet in earth nor heaven

Beats any heart more valiant or more pure.

He hath been tried and hath sore trial borne

As steel of surest temper, true at need,

Or as that asken spear from Pelion's woods,

His weapon huge that none may wield but he,

Peleus, the son of thy son whom erewhile

The daughter of the River, once thy love,

Bare thee on earth: on Peleus falls the lot,

To him this bride is given, but with her bears

A sign inseparable, which to learn

Shall leave ye well content to yield to-day

What might infer far sorer sacrifice.

Thus hath Fate spoken: whosoe'er he be

That weds the sea-maid Thetis, unto him,

Or man or God immortal, must she bear

A son that shall be mightier than his sire.

Kings of the sky and sea, mark well this word.

No more let Peleus for his God-wooed bride

Be envied, or if envied, only then

For lowliness that calms the fear of fall.

What hurt have men, brief beings of a day,

If thus their sons succeeding top their power?

No hurt but joy, to mark the younger fame

Build up the gathering glory of their race.

But if, coëval in undying prime,

Some mightier son, as needs the mightier must,

On trident or on lightning laid his hand,

With unimagined iteration dire

Rousing wild memories of an elder world,

Ruins and revolutions hidden deep

In Time's dark gulf whereto no eyes revert.

Far other deed were that, far other doom."

He ended, and the assembly all amazed

At that unlooked-for sentence, in great awe

On the two sovran Brethren bent their eyes.

No whit had either moved, but on the Seer

Kept their large gaze majestic, fixed and full.

Then, as one impulse in the twain had stirred,

From both with one accord their high assent

Rolled through the solemn stillness, deep and clear :

"So be it as thou sayest, Voice of Fate."

Therewith in confirmation those great Gods,

Immortal and imperial, bowed their brows.

Heaven stirred at that dread sign, and Earth afar

Thrice rocked responsive, heaving all her seas.

Again the Thunderer spake : "Titan, thy task

Is ended, but not ended be thy stay

Among thy peers, this company of Gods.

Here is thy place prepared, here dwell content,

Our counsellor at need, our new-won friend.

Rest here at ease, and learn the unfolded tale

By all these ages wrought in Heaven and Earth,

And changeful tribes of men, thy chosen care,

Once loved by thee alone; but now, be sure,

There is no God that hath not linked his name,

Perchance his race, to human hope and fear.

Stay then, for change by change is recompensed,

And new things now wax old, and old are new."

He spake, and all the approving throng divine

With acclamation free applauded loud,

Bidding the Titan welcome and all hail;

Henceforth, they cried, a counsellor of Heaven,

Interpreter of Fate, and friend of Man.

But when their greeting ceased, and sought reply,

He raised his eyes, and with slow-moving gaze

Looked round on that celestial company.

Then with deep voice and mild he answering said:

"Deem not, O Gods, I lightly prize your call.

Thought of inveterate wrong, no longer now

By hourly instant anguish riveted,

Hath fallen from my soul, and left her free

To sweep on ample circles of her wing

Amid dim visions, slowly growing clear,

Of rolling age on age, her proper realm,

Her proper lore ; yet all I gladly learn :

Either of this new kindlier life of Heaven,

Or of that once-scorned world of suffering men,

Whereto your world is linked for ever now,

Right gladly would I hear, yet not as one

Quite shut from knowledge all these exiled years.

Think ye my Mother dear, deep-murmuring Earth,

Could find no means of message, when I lay

On the bare rock between her breast and

　　Heaven ?—

That starry Heaven that made me know my life

Not unbefriended of celestial Powers,

Though other than Olympian ; year by year,

Through height ineffable of frozen air,

Stooped the keen stars, and graved upon my soul,

In fateful characters of golden fire,

Deep and more deep, their slow-unfolding lore.

And more of what they told I too must tell,

Sometime, not now: enough of things to be

Hath been to-day revealed. But now, O Gods,

Farewell; I may not tarry for your voice,

Your friendly voice; but other voices call,

Inaudible to you, but to this heart

Admonitory, o'ermastering, deeply dear.

Yea, my racked being yearns for great repose,

Deep sleep and sweet, almost the sleep of death:

And after that, long time my life must pause

In meditative musing, now no more

Pierced by abrupt assault of arrowy pain.

Not here my place of rest; far hence I seek,

Beyond or world of Gods or world of men,

The Tower of ancient Kronos, where he dwells

Amid the Blessed Isles, his final home,

The habitation of a holy calm.

There evermore the West-winds dewy-winged,

Borne o'er the Ocean-river, lightly breathe;

And over all that sweet and solemn realm

Broods a mild golden light of mellow beam,

Less bright by far than this celestial splendour,

A low warm light, as of eternal eve.

And there are gathered, or shall gather soon,

All my dear kindred, offspring of the Earth,

The brotherhood Titanic, finding there

Harbour desired, and after sore exile

Rejoining well content their ancient King.

Nor these alone; for to that saving shore

A race far other surely shall be called,

Of seed far humbler sprung, but by decree

Of dooms august, that doom both God and Man,

Raised to high meed, the spirits of just men

Made here companions of immortal Gods;

Themselves perchance—grudge not, O seed of

    Heaven !—

Destined, despite their clay, to conquer death.

There for long years, how long I know not yet,

My lot is fixed with that dear folk to dwell;

But not for ever; sometime yet to be

(Thus far I know and tell) I come again,

To counsel, and to do, and to endure.

But whether to this glorious hall of Heaven,

Or whether unto Man's long-suffering brood,

I know not—nay nor even surely know

If this my shape wherein I stand to-day

Be changed at my new coming: on such wise

Wears my great Mother many a form and name,

Yet holds through all her one identity.

Thus may I too. Or if the time shall come

When all the storèd counsel of my soul

Is spent, and all mine oracles outworn,

There shall not fail a prophet in my place,

Some hand to bear the torch, new wisdom bringing

Wiser than Promethéan; yet that too

Taught him not only by the all-teacher Time,

But by long toil and travail, hate and love,

Design, and disappointment, and defeat,

And by rapt converse held with Earth, and Stars,

And with deep hidden well-springs of the world.

But now to my much yearned for rest afar

I must begone.   Wherefore, for that long way,

I pray ye, deathless Presences of Heaven,

Suffer one moment in your shining halls

The appointed convoy that shall bear me hence.

They wait without, and now are near at hand.

My strength is spent in speaking: Gods, farewell."

He ceased, but with his word they saw descend

Two Shapes benign that with wide-hovering wing,

Noiseless as birds' that through the brooding night

Flit all unheard, and of like feathery form,

Close to the Titan's side came floating down.

Well known the one, and welcome even in Heaven,

For even in Heaven who shall not welcome Sleep?

But round his brother twin a halo hung,

Wellnigh invisible, a filmy veil,

And his calm lips were paler: through the Gods

A brief scarce-heeded shudder lightly ran

At that mild Presence, for they looked on Death.

Not for dominion came he there that day,

But helpmeet of his brother, bound with him

To welcome succour of the weary God.

So to his side those Forms fraternal drew.

His faint eyes half had closed, his failing head

Sank on the breast of Sleep: together both

Raised him with reverent touch, and spread their

   plumes

Inaudibly.   One beat of those wide wings,

Fraught with their sacred burden, bare them forth ;

And in a moment, lo, the heavenly hall

Held them no more, but far they fleeted on

Down through the glimmering deep of empty air.

I.

THE sea-sand who shall number,
  Or tell the wasted store
Of fallen leaves that cumber
  The wintry forest floor?

So dense, so all unthought for,
  Drop down in lane and den
From wretched life they wrought for
  The dying throngs of men.

Down drop they bruised and breathless,
  Forget at last to feel:
Above the dead men deathless
  Fate drives her iron wheel.

c

No ray for these arisen

  Had pledged a glimpse of day ;

To break their sunless prison

  This was the only way.

II.

Blow strong, blow sweet, O Ocean wind,

  As o'er the Ocean waves we flee !

Sweep forth the old life from our mind,

  Inspire the life to be !

There Nature shares her godlike moods,

  Stars in a clearer heaven are there ;

The glory of the flaming woods,

  The glory of the air.

The elder lands that seemed so wide,

  Now all too straitly, sorely pen,

Too close for kindness, side by side,

    The jostling lives of men.

Behind us, lo, the landward light,

  Choked by the mist, forlorn and grey,

Has paled and past, forsaking quite

    The portals of the day.

But yonder, lo, the fervid skies

  Flood with their fire the western brine;

'Tis there our spirits' sun shall rise,

    Some unknown day divine.

BEYOND the ages far away,

    When yet the fateful Earth was young,

And mid her seas unfurrowed lay

    Her lands uncitied and unsung,

The Gods in council round their King

Were met for her apportioning.

Then shook the Sire the golden urn

    Wherefrom the lots leapt forth to view,

And God by God took up in turn

    The symbol of his kingdom due;

Till each had linked some heavenly name

To human hope and human fame.

When lo, a footstep on the floor,

    A radiance in the radiant air;

A God august, forgot before,

    Too late arrived, was lastly there—

The Sun-god from his fiery car

Unyoked beneath the evening star.

Then said the Sire: "For thee no lot,

    O Sun, of all the lots is drawn,

For thy bright chariot, well I wot,

    Hath held thee since the broadening dawn.

But come, for all the gods are fain

For thy fair sake to cast again."

" Nay now, for me is little need

    New lots to cast" (so spake the Sun);

" One isle assign me for the meed

    Of that diurnal course I run:

Behold beneath the glimmering sea

A land unclaimed, the land for me."

Therewith he shot an arrowy ray

    Down through the blue Aegean deep;

Thrilled by that magic dart of day,

    The hidden isle shook off her sleep.

She moved, she rose, and with the morn

She touched the air, and Rhodes was born.

Then all about that starry sea

   There ran a gratulating stir,

Her fellows for all time to be

   In choral congress greeting her,

With air-borne song and flashing smiles,

A sisterhood of glorious isles.

And still as from his car on high

   Her Lord his daily splendour sent,

She joyed to know his gladdening eye

   On her, his best-beloved, was bent:

And ever in that fostering gaze

Grew up the stature of her praise.

What early wondrous might was hers,

    The craftsmanship of cunning hands,

Of that wise art the harbingers

    Whose fame is uttered through all lands

Then Rhodians by the Sun-god's side

Besought Athene to abide.

She came, she loved the Rosy Isle,

    And Lindos reared her eastward fane

To Rhodian chiefs she brought the while

    New thoughts, new valiance in her train,

New hope to bind about their brows

The olive of her Father's house.

Then won Diagoras that prize

   Yet fairer than his silvery crown,

That voice whereby in godlike wise

   His name through time goes deathless down.

In graven gold her walls along

Flamed forth the proud Pindaric song.

She too her own Athenians stirred

   To that fair deed of chivalry,

That high imperishable word

   That set the Rhodian Dorieus free,

And linked in unison divine

Her Lindian to her Attic shrine.

Bright hours, too brief! The shadowing hand

    Half barbarous of a giant form

Even the strong Sun-god's loyal land

    Must wrap in mist of sombre storm,

When Hellas bowed, her birthright gone,

Beneath the might of Macedon.

Yet even then not lightly bound

    Was Rhodes of any vanquisher;

With all his engines thundering round

    The City-stormer[1] stormed not her.

In vain: anon the Roman doom

Had sealed her spirit in the tomb.

        [1] Demetrius Poliorcetes.

Long ages slept she.   Then a dream

   Once more across her slumber shone,

Cleaving the dark, a quickening gleam

   All-glorious as in days foregone;

A new God's presence nobler far

Than any Lord of sun or star.

He showed her him whose chosen head

   Had leaned upon his holy breast;

" For John my well-beloved," he said,

   " Stand forth, a champion of the West,

Sealed with my name, and his in mine,

Our vanguard in the war divine."

She rose, she stemmed the Moslem flood

    That roared and ravined for her life,

Till drop by drop the knightly blood

    Was drained in that stupendous strife;

Then, sole amid the o'erwhelming sea,

Sank in heroic agony.

'Twice born, twice slain! all this is o'er

    Three hundred years; yet may there be

(So strong a life is in thy core),

    O Rhodes, another birth for thee.

Look up, behold this banner new,

The white cross on the field of blue.

Through all the Isles the broadening light

   Creeps on its sure but lingering way,

And half are in the fading night

   And half are in the dawning day:

Thou too, O Rhodes, shalt make thee one

Once more with freedom and the Sun.

HERMES WITH THE CHILD
BACCHUS.

(A statue made by Praxiteles, and lately disinterred at
Olympia.)

FROM the dim North, from Danube's stream
unknown,

Behind the blast of winter, where abide

The Hyperborean folk, a mystic land,

Came Heracles, and bare the silvery bough

To shade the plain beside Alpheus' bed,

And be a crown of valiance evermore.

Therefore through all the golden prime of
Earth,

When her best race was glad beneath the day,

Endured that praise; and as of stars the Sun

Is first, and Gold of metals, as of all

Earth's primal gifts to man is Water best,

So he who spake for understanding ears

Words of divine assignment, crowns of song,

Of all fair feasts the Olympic deemed most fair.

   Here was the home of Zeus, the shrines were

      here

Of Gods and sons of Gods, his lineage high,

So many ages worshipt where they dwelt,

So many ages after, all forgot;

Whether their carven forms by robber hands

Were rapt beyond the sea, or ground to dust,

Or whether in the kindly breast of Earth

Patient they slept, even as dead bones of men.

Sleeping or dead alike they sank from sight,

And through the ages no man recked to mourn

For their mild brows and presence tutelar,

Similitude divine, divinely wrought.

But now once more with keen remorseful eyes,

And hunger of the heart for beauty dead,

Men seek them sorrowing, and with painful hands

Upturn the sacred soil till, maimed and rare,

Strange clouded fragments of the ancient glory,

Late lingerers of the company divine,

Arise, like glimmering phantoms of a dream.

Yet even in ruin of their marble limbs

They breathe of that far world wherefrom they

    came,

Of liquid light and harmonies serene,

Lost halls of Heaven and large Olympian air.

Thus slept He long, thus hath He risen so late,

The Son of Maia: that the earth no more

Holds him in night sepulcral, this to him

Is nought, or eyes of gazers; his own world

He bears within him, all untoucht of Time.

Yet haply if thou gaze upon the God

In reverent silence, even to thee shall flow

From that high presence of the unconscious form

Some effluent spell, whereby thy calmèd soul

Shall be indrawn to that diviner world

Wherein his soul hath being, fair and free.

Unharmed of chance and ruin, lo, his head

Bends with half-smile benign above his charge,

The little child, the son of Semele,

Snatched from the fierce tongues of celestial fire,

The insupportable blaze of very Zeus,

His mother's doom; but from his baby soul

The terror of that night hath passed away,

And left him blithe on his mild brother's arm,

His tender hand on that strong shoulder prest.

Hermes, was this thy gift? Yet well thou knewest

D

How wild a sway that babe full-grown would wield,

The God of frenzied brain and blood afire,

Fired howsoe'er divinely: yea, but thou

Could'st turn these too to glory and delight,

Spirit more pure and loftier life of man.

For thou into man's teeming thoughts pent up,

And inarticulate fancies, didst inbreathe

Voice like thine own ; and passion's tuneless storm

Sweeping therethrough made sudden melodies,

The sweeter for its frenzy, for from thee

Came spells of song and speech, from thee the lyre.

And where the pillared city's festal folk

In sunny mart or shadowed portico

Were met for converse, or where athlete youth

In emulous games honoured the all-giving Gods,

And native Earth, and immemorial power

Of quickening Rivers that right well had reared

Their growing manhood, thy grave smile was there.

Interpreter of Heaven, these were not all,

Not all thy gifts, though plenteous; nay, though
   these

Be very good, yet one, the best, remains.

For thou, fair lord, thou also, having filled

Man's little life so full with act and thought,

Leadest him lastly down the darkling road

To that dim realm where griefs and gains are dead,

Or live as dreams dreamed by a dream-like shade.

Were they indeed aught more beneath the noon

Of this brave Sun that must himself wax cold?

Who knoweth? Come, dear Guardian, Guide
   divine;

For this thou art arisen out of earth

That held thee there in Elis sleeping well.

Give thou the babe to Rhea; she no less,

Mysterious Mother of an elder Heaven,

Hath store of spells to heal the coming gust

Of his young madness; take thy serpent-wand,

And gather to thee those thy subject souls

Born out of due time in an alien world,

To whom are given, in toil or in repose,

So rare, so faint, thine advent and thine aid.

They shall not shrink or flutter, as the ghosts

Of those impure the avenging arrows slew,

But follow firmly on, until they come

To some fair congress of the noble dead,

Set free from flying pain and flying joy,

There find their home, and rest for ever there.

ACHILLES.

A THWART the sunrise of our western day

    The form of great Achilles, high and clear,

    Stands forth in arms, wielding the Pelian spear.

The sanguine tides of that immortal fray,

Swept on by Gods, around him surge and sway,

    Wherethrough the helms of many a warrior peer,

    Strong men and swift, their tossing plumes

        uprear.

But stronger, swifter, goodlier he than they,

More awful, more divine. Yet mark anigh ;

    Some fiery pang hath rent his soul within,

    Some hovering shade his brows encompasseth.

What gifts hath Fate for all his chivalry ?

    Even such as hearts heroic oftenest win ;

    Honour, a friend, anguish, untimely death.

MAZZINI AND GARIBALDI.

IMMORTAL Brethren, saviour spirits fair,
    Ye were not born to your dear land alone;
    Earth's golden book enrolls you as her own,
And of your honour all the world is heir.
For in an age sunk deep in sordid care
    Ye still had ears to list a nobler tone,
    Ye called to loyal hearts, and led them on,
Loyal to love, disdainful of despair.

The earthquake and the thunder and the fire,
    These in your godlike struggle clothed you o'er,
And clouds confused of lurid vapour dire.
    Now in the firmament's untroubled floor
Shine your twin stars whereto our souls aspire,
    Moved with the moving heaven for evermore.

FOLKESTONE CLIFF.

(On the projected Tunnel under the Channel.)

"LET there be Sea," God said, and there was
    Sea ;
  And in the midst thereof an Island set,
  Wherein the roving strength of nations met,
And reared a rugged fortress of the free.
"Take back thy Sea," men say, if men they be
  Who thus their fathers' perilous years forget,
  Nor reck the gathering thunder-cloud, which yet
Looms large from many an envious tyranny.

Gropers for gold, come forth! Let be awhile
  The stifling dark of your disloyal mine :
Here where no feverish fumes the sense beguile,
  Where reinless waves race by in endless line,
Here stand! Behind you lies the guarded Isle,
  And on your brows beats free the guardian brine.

ON THE DEATH OF JAMES SPEDDING

(Expositor and defender of Francis Bacon).

FAREWELL, benignant spirit, mild and wise,
That wert like some still lake among the hills
Of thy fair home ancestral, fed by rills
That stir unseen its deep translucencies.
Beneath the patient gaze of those calm eyes
The inveterate crust of errors and of ills
That clings around the past, and clinging kills,
Fell off, and earth through thee had fewer lies.

To serve one honoured Shade thy life was planned,
Riches past by, the noise of fame unheard;
For this not over-rashly may we dare
To rank thee with the royal-hearted band
Upon whose brows is writ the undying word:
Not hate but love this soul was born to share [1].

March, 1881.

[1] οὔτοι συνέχθειν ἀλλὰ συμφιλεῖν ἔφυν.—*Antigone.*

THE BAY OF LERICI.

LEAP, wildly leap, Ligurian sea,
  Where Shelley on his wandering way,
Ere thy embraces set him free,
  Made his last halt in earthly day.

Low on the beach I see it stand,
  Flecked by the flying shreds of foam,
A mourner on that magic strand,
  Shut up and sealed, his lonely home.

Beyond the headland to and fro
  Italia's mail-clad navies glide;
Their gallant crews nor reck nor know
  That here a poet dwelt and died.

Yet if they knew it, might they own

   Some debt, howe'er remote, to one

Whose voice with sterner voices blown

   About the world, beneath a sun

Mocked evermore by human night,

   Called to the slaves of sloth and fear

To wake, to strive, for lo, the light,

   Unseen, unhoped for, drew anear.

No throne of intellectual state

   Held him from men apart, above;

Nor thought nor art nor life could sate

   That soul whose longing was for love.

Earth's ill could cloud but not deform

   His spirit born for gentler air,

As even now a transient storm

   Marred this bright bay, divinely fair.

But lo, the drifted clouds divide,

   The glad spring sunlight glimmering through,

The hurrying waves forget to chide,

   A rainbow fades into the blue.

*   *   *   *   *

Ah haply, far from wrath and wrong,

   Finds he, where never loves grow dim,

That answer to his Ariel-song

   No earthly voice might render him?

VALLOMBROSA.

ENGLISH wanderer, where Etruria sings to thee

    Songs of mountain and of forest fair,

Each clear stream with its beech-leaf burden brings
to thee

    Days long flown, wherein Milton wandered there.

Scenes youth lit for his ardour and his purity

    Age raised up when his outer eye was dim:

Vallombrosa, thy name through all futurity

    Blends sweet tones with a sweeter tone from him.

HIGH STREET FELL, WESTMORELAND.

(So called from bearing traces of a Roman road.)

IMPERIAL Rome, whose footprint sparsely seen

    Stamps the wide face of thy devolved demesne,

Whose mighty works in mighty ruin hurled

Lie rare and crumbling o'er the western world;

Where'er thy circling galleries now no more

Echo to beast and man their murderous roar;

Or where thy conquering arches high and far

Bestride the grey bed of the wondering Gard:—

Here too, even here, high on our lonely fell,

The paven mountains of thy presence tell.

Here where the red deer roam, the curlews cry,

The Italian watchword rang beneath the sky:

Here in proud march, the indignant dales above,

Flashed the bronze birds of Capitolian Jove:

Here to rapt thought thy Phantom shall arise,

A faded light of lordship in her eyes,

And by sad gaze in silence eloquent

Charge on our race her dread admonishment:

" The word of Rome to Britain, queen to queen;

Would'st thou still be? Be not what I have been.

What though far nations in the shadowing awe

Of thy wide rule lie lapt in peace and law,

Earth-girdling armies shall no whit avail

In thy dark hour, if in thyself thou fail.

Boast not thine arms that stretch so large and
    long,

The heart, the heart—that keep thou pure and
    strong!

Let not the world, let not God mourn once
    more

A giant empire cankered at the core."

THE KINGDOM OF LOVE.

I.

THE SANCTUARY.

THE shepherd lover of old Sicily,

   Singing sweet song, sweet in all pain's despite,

   Before the cave that hid his love from sight,

Would fain have been the tawny mountain-bee,

That on like honey-seeking wing might he

      Flit in beneath the hanging ivy bright

      And tremulous fern, and fly to his Delight;

Even her for whom his soul longed lovingly.

Mine is that bliss and more, for while I roam

   Through the strange world, my soul one image

         bears ,

   Of one still cave, one bridal sanctuary,

Where Love and Truth and Beauty make their home

   In one dear Form, and make my home with

         theirs,

      Builded for these and me immovably.

E

II.

AN ANNIVERSARY.

SWEET heart, this day a year ago our lives
   for ever blended,

   We knelt beneath the ancient rite, we vowed
      the ancient vow:

Now joyful hope is merged in joy, and dream
   by deed transcended,

   The spring that welled so brightly then, runs
      a bright river now.

That day, from inmost heaven sent, a Spirit stood
    before us,

  His wings were lit with rainbow light, and on
    his brow a star :

A wand with dews of Eden wet he bare, and
    waved it o'er us,

  At his sweet summons forth we went, and
    followed him afar.

Through wondrous ways, by earthly guides un-
    trodden, undiscovered,

  He led us on, in trust and joy still following
    hand in hand :

A thousand happy mated birds amid the wood-
    land hovered,

  The very earth with gladness heaved, and
    gleamed with golden sand.

Sometimes within those fairy glades, those dreamy
    deep recesses,
  Almost thy gentle heart had failed, so strangely
    fair they seemed,
But evermore new faith grew up to meet new-
    found caresses,
  And still within the magic shade the star
    benignant beamed.

It paused amid the pine-forest; we lay in awe
    and wonder;
  The birds were hushed; a silence fell; we
    listened long and long:
Then softly through that holy place, around, above,
    and under,
  Came murmuring on a solemn sound, the pine-
    wood's secret song.

We left the glen, we sought the sun ; but that
high hour had brought us
A charm through all our lives to live, an
undersong sublime :
For Love our lord, our spirit-guide, his master-
spell had taught us,
The spell he knows and he alone, the spell
that conquers Time.

III.

DAWN.

HOW soft thy rosy fingers fall,
  Fair Dawn, upon the happy eyes
Where Love their lord, their all in all,
  Dwells and makes glad his votaries;

A steadfast Love, with folded wings
  That spread to flee no more, no more,
But fan with mystic murmurings
  The deathless flame whose seed they bore.

How mild the sounds of morning come,
  Whether around some rural bower,
Or even the city's gathering hum
  Is hallowed by the magic hour.

Her fairy head has felt the Dawn,

   And stirs, unwakened, till it rest,

By sweet unconscious impulse drawn,

   On the broad pillow of my breast.

Ah, gladness pure as moorland dew!

   What golden word might e'er express

The still deep joy that thrills me through,

   Unfathomable tenderness?

Two wingëd presences divine

   Above our guarded rest maintain

Their interwoven watch benign,

   To link the hours with charmëd chain.

We feel amid the silence deep

   Their brooding plumage gently move;

Love laid us on the wings of Sleep,

   And Sleep has borne us back to Love.

IV.

THE ROSE.

A ROSE I bear close-cherished in my breast,
  Nurtured on earth, but all her being fair
So bathed in dews of heaven and heavenly air
That of sweet magic is she grown possest,
In new unfolding petals ever drest,
  And ever breathing some new fragrance rare;
  Whereto my heart must fondly still repair
To feed my inmost life and tenderest.

Yet through all varying charm my starry rose
  Denies no whit her dear identity.
    One peerless perfume hers, one crimson
      flame
Through infinite new birth of beauty glows;
  Through all love past and all sweet love to be,
    Changeless in change, for evermore the same.

THE RIVER OF LOVE.

L O the River from the blue hills welling,

    Stream of Love that ever stronger rolls,

Stronger, sweeter, higher and higher swelling,

    Bears for ever our entwinëd souls.

Close embraced in bonds no shock can sunder

    Fare we, well content whate'er befall:

Let the changeful skies or smile or thunder:

    Storm and sunshine—we have heart for all.

Somewhere, well we know, in ambush lying

    Right athwart our River, near or far,

Gorged with hopes engulfed, our hope defying,

    Death, the sandbank, rears his gloomy bar.

Then shall our brave River, swiftlier sweeping,

    Burst the bar and o'er it bear us free,

Out and onward to the Ocean leaping,

    Out and on to Love's eternal sea.

VERSIONS

FROM

HOMER'S ILIAD

AND VIRGIL'S AENEID.

THE ANGERING OF ACHILLES.

(Homer's *Iliad* i. 1-305.)

OF the ruinous wrath of Achilles thy song, O
Goddess, shall tell,

Wherethrough to the army Achaian unnumbered
sorrows befell,

And heroes many and strong were sent down to
the Lord of the dead,

Ghosts, while the carrion birds and the dogs on
their carcases fed,

From the hour when sundering strife—thus Zeus
was achieving his plan—

Of the monarch of men, Agamemnon and godlike
Achilles began.

What God was the cause of their strife? Even
  He whom Leto of yore

Bare unto Zeus. He it was who sent in his
  anger sore

Plague thro' the host of Achaians; their warriors
  wasted away

For the wrong that the king Agamemnon to
  Chryses wrought on the day

When he came to the ships of Achaians to ransom
  his daughter dear.

In his hands were the wreaths of the God, of
  Apollo the Far-darter,

Bound on a golden wand; and he prayed to
  the host in his pain:

All the Achaians he prayed, but chief the Atri-
  dae twain:

  "Children of Atreus, and ye, well-greavèd
  Achaians, hear!

Unto you may the Lords of Olympus give up to
 be spoil of your spear

This city of Priam ye war with, and bring you in
 joy to your land ;

But loose ye the child of my love, and take her
 price from my hand,

Fearing the Son of the Highest, Apollo the Lord
 of the Bow."

 Then fain had they honoured the priest and
 taken the price even so :

But the thing displeased Agamemnon, and fiercely
 he drave him away.

 " Never again, old man, let me find thee henceforth from this day,

Lest the wreaths and the wand of Apollo avail
 not to shield thee from ill.

Her will I never give back ; in my palace
 abiding still

Growing old in the Argive land far away from
    her home she shall bide,
Weaving the woof at the loom and sharing my
    couch by my side.
Go, and arouse not my wrath, that no harm
    light here on thy head."
  He spake, and the old man obeyed, and past
    from his presence in dread,
Silently on by the beach, by the thundering surge
    of the sea;
And he called on his Lord, on Apollo, and prayed
    to him fervently:
  "God of the silver bow, in whom Chryse and
    Killa delight,
Hear me, O Sminthian Prince, that in Tenedos
    rulest with might!
Lo, if I ever have reared thee a shrine that seemed
    fair in thine eyes,

Ever have burnt on thine altar a savoury
 sacrifice,

Thigh-bones of bulls and of goats—fulfil me this
 thing that I pray!

Be my tears on the host of Achaians avenged by
 thine arrows to-day!"

   So prayed he, and Phoebus Apollo gave ear to
 the old man's cry.

Wroth in his heart he arose, and went down from
 Olympus on high:

On his back were his bow and his quiver, the
 arrows rattled aloud.

Dark as the night he descended, and sate him
 apart from the crowd

Of the ships and the army around: then he shot,
 and the silver bow

Clanged with a terrible clang as the arrow bounded
 below.

First on the mules and the dogs and next on
the warriors sped
Shaft upon shaft, and more thickly burnt ever the
pyres of the dead.
Nine days long from Apollo descended his
darts thro' the fleet;
On the tenth day Achilles arose, and he summoned
the people to meet.
White-armed Here the Goddess had set this thought
in his breast,
For she grieved for the Danaän host when she
saw how they fell in the pest.
Then when they gathered in council, Achilles
arose, and he said:
"Back must we travel, methinks, Agamemnon,
back to our home;
For who shall be left with his life when both battle
and pestilence come?

Lo, let us ask of a seër, a prophet who speaketh
aright—

Yea, a diviner of dreams, for of God come dreams
of the night—

Let him say whether Phoebus Apollo hath lacked
from us aught of his due,

Prayer or sacrifice haply, that thus his anger
we rue.

Sheep then and goats we will give him if these
he lacketh, to burn

On his altar, if so from our comrades his terrible
arrows he turn."

   Thus having spoken he sate. Then Kalchas
rose in his place,

Kalchas, Thestor's son, a diviner the best of his
race ;

Present and past he knew, and the things that
were fated to be :

The Achaian ships he had guided to Ilios over
the sea

All of his subtle divining, the gift of Apollo his
Lord.

Now he arose in the midst, and of goodwill uttered
his word :

"The cause of the wrath of Apollo thou bidd'st
me, Achilles, declare.

Therefore that cause will I tell.   But do thou first
pledge me and swear

That with tongue and with arm thou wilt aid me if
one shall be wroth at my tale,

One whom the Argives give ear to, a chieftain of
mighty avail.

Heavy the hand of a king, if his wrath on a
weaker alight,

For though for the day he refrain him and smother
his anger from sight,

Yet deep in his heart it abideth and lieth in wait
     to do harm,

Tarrying long. Say then, dost thou pledge me
     the shield of thine arm?"

   Then swift-foot Achilles made answer : " Say out
     Heaven's will without fear.

By the God whom thou servest I swear it, Apollo
     to Zeus most dear,

None, while I live on the earth and look forth
     with these eyes on the light,

By the hollow ships shall come nigh thee, O Kalchas,
     to do thee despite :

No, none of the Danaän army, not though
     Agamemnon be he,

Who far above all the Achaians the chiefest avows
     him to be."

   Then the prophet took heart when he heard him,
     and spake at Achilles' desire :

" Hecatomb nowise nor vow is the cause of Apollo's
    ire,

But the wrong to the priest of his altar, whose
    child Agamemnon hath ta'en

And denieth the prayer of her father to yield her
    for ransom again.

Therefore the Archer Apollo hath sent these woes,
    and will send,

Ruthless, nor ever this evil among our host have
    an end,

Till we give back the maid to her father unbought,
    without ransom or fine,

And a hecatomb send unto Chryse ; so turn we
    the anger divine."

  Thus having spoken he sate.   Then arose
    Agamemnon in ire ;

Filled was his heart with his fury, his eyes as the
    flame of a fire.

Terribly looked he on Kalchas, and spake to him :
" Prophet of ill,

Never a good thing yet hast thou told me, for
ever thy will

Evil to prophesy only, and now thou must rise
and divine

How the wrath of Apollo is kindled because
Chryseïs is mine,

And I took not her price from her father but
held her in honoured thrall.

Yea so, and I deem Clytemnestra, the wedded wife
of my hall,

No whit better in beauty or wisdom or skill of her
hand.

Yet, for all this, will I yield her, if thus doth
our welfare demand,

Loth that the people should perish : but give me
a prize in her place,

That I be not alone of Achaians bereft of such
token of grace.

For now ye behold me dishonoured and lorn of
the prize that I won."

Then answered him swift-foot Achilles, " Thou
famous man, Atreus' son,

Covetous heart above all ! what know we of spoil
in our store

Whence to allow thee a prize? All the spoil was
apportioned before,

Not to be now begged back. To Apollo the
maiden restore,

And to thee will the army Achaian pay recompense
manifold more,

Whensoever shall Zeus to our onset some town
of the Trojans assign."

Then the lord Agamemnon made answer
" Not thus, though all valour be thine,

Not thus, O thou godlike Achilles, thy word shall

    outwit me by guile.

Dost thou think thou shalt keep thine own guerdon,

    and I sit dishonoured the while,

Bidding me lightly restore her? Nay, if the

    Achaians allot

Recompense meet to my mind, not a meaner

    thing, well: but if not,

Then will I seize it myself, nor take heed tho'

    the owner be thou—

Thou or Odysseus or Aias, nor reck for the

    wrath on his brow.

This for our after providing: now launch we a

    ship on the deep,

Man her with rowers to row, and her hold with

    a hecatomb heap,

And send on her fair-faced Chryseïs; and one

    of our chieftains withal,

Idomeneus, Aias, Odysseus; or, yet more noble
than all,

Even thyself, O Achilles, shalt order the journey
and lead,

Giving sacrifice meet to the God, that the folk
from his anger be freed."

Grim was the gaze of Achilles as straightway
he answered again :

"O in shamelessness clad as a garment, most
greedy and guileful of men,

Shall yet an Achaian be found who for thy sake
shall journey or fight?

For no quarrel of mine with the Trojans came I :
they had touched not my right :

Neither oxen nor horses of mine had they ever
yet harried for spoil,

Nor ever in populous Phthia, my land of the
bountiful soil,

Wasted the fruits of the earth; for between their
country and mine

Stretch many shadowy mountains and roaring
billows of brine.

But thee, O thou dog-face, we follow, and fight
with the spearmen of Troy

To avenge Menelaüs thy brother and win for
thee honour and joy.

Nought of all this hast thou recked, yea, now
from my keeping wouldst tear

The meed the Achaians assigned me, the meed
of sore travail I bare.

Ay, and whene'er the Achaians have stormed
some fortress at bay,

These hands bear the brunt of the battle, but
when we take shares of the prey,

Ampler by far is thy portion, while I some
remnant of spoil,

Little but dear, carry back for reward of my
warfare and toil.

Now with my ships will I homeward, for this
seemeth better by far

Than here in dishonour abiding to win thee
wealth from the war."

Then the lord Agamemnon made answer:
"Yea flee, if so falleth thy will.

Never thine aid will I crave; there be others to
honour me still,

Zeus above all. Of all kings thou art ever most
hateful to me:

Ever thy joy is in strife and in battle. Tho'
mighty thou be,

God's gift surely is this. Now home with thy
Myrmidons hie:

Lord it there among them. Of thine anger right
heedless am I.

Yea and I promise thee this: since the God

    Chryseïs demands,

Her in my ship send I back; but instead will

    I seize with my hands

Even thy prize, Briseïs, and thus shalt thou know

    to thy pain

How I am greater than thou, and none else

    shall defy me again."

    He said, and Achilles in anguish made question

    within with his heart

Whether with drawn sword rising to scatter the

    Council apart

And slay Agamemnon before them, or whether

    his wrath to assuage.

Thus while he doubted distraught, and unsheathed

    the great sword in his rage,

Down came Athene from heaven, and laid her

    grasp on his hair—

White-armed Here had sent her, for both those
kings were her care.

None but Achilles beheld her—none else might
the Goddess espy—

And he turned him about in amazement, and knew
the dread light in her eye.

And he spake to her: "Daughter of Zeus, wherefore comest thou hither to-day?

Is it to look on the pride of Atrides? Now this
will I say—

Ay, and my word shall be deed—for his scorn
shall he yield me his life."

But the bright-eyed Goddess made answer: " Full
fain would I soften the strife,

If haply to me thou wilt hearken, for now am I
come from above,

Sent by the white-armed Here—of both ye twain
she hath love.

Draw not thy sword from his sheath, but rebuke
     with upbraiding the king.

Lo, I foretell thee a truth whereof time the fulfil-
     ment shall bring;

Threefold gifts shall be thine for this wrong's sake ;
     but hearken us now!"

  Then swift-foot Achilles made answer: "The
     bidding that Here and thou

Lay on a man, must he hearken, tho' fiercely the
     wrath in him burn.

Whoso hath hearkened the Gods, unto him give
     they hearing in turn."

  He said, and the weight of his hand on the silver
     hilt of his sword

Stayed, and thrust back to the sheath, for he
     hearkened Athene's word.

  She to Olympus departed, and entered the house
     of her Sire.

But fierce was Achilles' rebuke, as he spake once
    more in his ire :
  " Heavy with wine, with the face of a dog and
    the heart of a hare !
Never to arm thee for battle among thy folk dost
    thou dare,
Never with princes Achaian from ambush to leap
    on the foe.
Better it booteth by far thro' the host of thy people
    to go
Seizing the meeds of their honour, if any withstand
    thee in aught,
King that devourest thy people !—a people whose
    manhood is naught,
Else had this wrong been thy last.   Now hearken
    the oath that I swear.
Yea, by this staff in my hand will I swear it, that
    never shall bear

Leaves neither twigs, for the mountains that nursed
it may know it no more,

Since the bronze of the axe hath bereft it of bark
and of leaves that it wore,

And the sons of Achaians in judgment, that guard
the traditions divine,

Wield it on high ; therefore mighty the oath that
is sworn on this sign.

Verily cometh a time when on all the Achaians
too late

Longing shall fall for Achilles, and then—tho' thy
anguish be great

When thou seëst thy people around thee by man-
slaying Hector's hand

Dying in heaps—not a whit shall thy impotent
succour withstand :

Nay, but with anger remorseful the heart in thy
breast shall be torn

G

That what time thy best man was beside thee thou

   dealtest him nought but thy scorn."

  Thus said Achilles in wrath, and the gold-studded

   staff to the ground

Hurled, and sat down; and in wrath Agamemnon

   fronting him frowned.

Then did the King of the Pylians, the clear-voiced

   Nestor, arise.

Sweeter than honey his speech; and already had

   past from his eyes

Two generations of men, and had left him king of

   the third.

Moved by good will to the chiefs he arose, and thus

   uttered his word:

  " Verily now to Achaians there cometh a ter-

   rible woe.

Priam and Priam's children and all that folk of

   the foe

Now shall have joy in their hearts, when they
    hear of the anger to-day

Risen between you twain, our first in the council
    and fray.

Nay, be advised; ye are younger than I; and yet
    mightier men

Once were my fellows, and scorned not my words :
    yea never again

Men shall I see such as Dryas, and great Poly-
    phemus of old,

Kaineus, Peirithoüs, Theseus, the mightiest whose
    deeds have been told.

Mightiest were they themselves and aye with the
    mightiest fought—

Monsters wild of the mountains—and gloriously
    brought them to naught.

These were my fellows of old, when I came out
    of Pylos afar,

Came, for they called me to come, and I fought
    my best in their war.

There is none might contend with those heroes
    of all in the world of to-day;

And all of them heeded my counsel, nor turned
    from my warning away.

So do ye also give heed. Therefore thou, Agamem-
    non, refrain

This damsel, the prize that we gave him, to wrest
    from Achilles again;

Neither do thou, O Achilles, be fain to contend
    with our Head.

Never as yet was there king on whom Zeus such
    glory hath shed.

Mighty in battle art thou, and the son of a mother
    divine,

But more are the men that he leads, and his power
    is greater than thine.

Therefore to cease from his anger alike Agamem-
    non I pray,

And Achilles the shield of Achaians, who beareth
    the brunt of the fray."

    Then made answer the King Agamemnon:
    " Yea, father, thou speakest aright,

But this man over all would prevail, over all he
    would brandish his might,

Master and lord over all; but his pride may no
    longer be borne:

Do the Gods, that have made him a warrior, for
    this give us up to his scorn?"

    Then answered in anger Achilles: " A coward
    and slave should I be

If in all thy behests I obeyed thee; for this seek
    another than me.

Thus further I bid thee to hearken, and ponder
    the word that I say:

Neither on thee nor another my hand shall be
    lifted to slay,

For sake of the damsel ye gave me ; ye gave,
    and ye take her away.

But of all my possessions beside, by my black
    swift ship by the sea,

Nothing of these shalt thou plunder or seize in
    defiance of me.

Nay, if thou darest, essay it, that these men may
    see it and fear :

Swiftly and surely thy life-blood shall gush round
    the point of my spear."

    Then from the strife of their speech they arose,
    and a little forbore,

And all the assembly Achaian was scattered abroad
    on the shore.

II.

THE ENMITY OF JUNO.

(Virgil's *Aeneid* i. 1–156.)

A RMS and the man I sing who first from Troy

    To Italy and coasts Lavinian came,

Predestined exile, over land and sea

Tossed to and fro long years by power divine,

To glut fierce Juno's unforgetful ire ;

Long too in war bested, till he might found

His City, and his Gods ancestral bear

To Latium, whence arose the Latin race,

And Alban sires, and walls of sovran Rome.

    Tell me the cause, O Muse, for what wrong done

To her divinity, what old offence,

Heaven's Queen so drave a man in duteous life

Pre-eminent, through countless toils and woe:

Dwells wrath so deep in hearts of heavenly line?

   There was an ancient City, Carthage called,

Daughter of Tyre, to Italy afar

Looking across the sea, and Tiber mouth ;

A City of wealth and fierce in works of war.

Juno, men say, above all other lands

Loved this, and ranked it before Samos' self ;

Here was her armour's shrine, her chariot here :

These walls, if Fate in anywise allow,

Even then she nursed to be the nations' head.

Yet had she heard how from the Trojan blood

A seed should spring to smite the Tyrian towers,

And thence for Libya's ruin should go forth

A race imperial, terrible in war :

So ran the doom of Fate.   Thereof in fear,

And mindful of that war her hand of old

For her belovëd Argos waged at Troy—

Ay, bitter memories of the ancient feud

Wounded her yet, that in her inmost soul

Deep-stored remained undying—Paris' choice,

Her beauty slighted, ravished Ganymede,

And all the hated tribe.—Stung by these griefs

Far off from Latium, tossed from sea to sea,

She drave the Trojan remnant left to live

By fell Achilles and the Danaän host:

Long years they roamed the seas, their destined

    doom.

Such toil it took to found the Roman race.

  Scarce out of sight of the Sicilian shore

They spread sail gladly for the open main,

Dashing the salt foam from their brazen prows,

When Juno, bearing still within her breast

Deep-driven her irremediable wound,

Thus with herself: "Must I from mine emprise

Hold baffled, nor avail to bar the road.

That leads the Trojan king to Italy?

The Fates forsooth forbid me! Did not Pallas

For one man's crime, Oïlean Ajax' frenzy,

Blast Argos' fleet and whelm the crews in death?

She darting from the clouds Jove's flying fire

Scattered the ships and tore the sea with storm;

Ajax, flames gasping from his cloven breast,

She in a hurricane caught up and hurled

On deadly rocks, impaled. But I, who move

The Queen of Heaven, Jove's sister and his wife,

With this one tribe these many years wage war.

Can any then still worship Juno's name,

Or grace in prayer her altars with a gift?"

    Such thought revolving in her heart afire

Unto the storm-clouds' realm the Goddess came,

The teeming home of wild winds of the South,

Aeolia. Here, within a cavern huge,

O'er roaring gales and tempests turbulent

King Aeolus bears sway, and curbs their fury

With prison-house and bonds. They round their

    den

Ever with awful murmur of the mount

Range wrathful: Aeolus the while above

In his high citadel the sceptre wields,

Their rage restraining: else, but for his guard,

Sea, earth, the very firmament of heaven,

In one wild ruin rapt, their wings would sweep.

That to prevent, the almighty Father's will

Pent them with pilëd hills in caverns dark,

A king ordaining, who by hest should know

Both when to tighten rein and when relax.

To whom thus Juno suppliant: "Aeolus,

For that the Sire of Gods and King of men

To thee gave powers to rouse the seas with storm

Or calm them—mark, a race mine ancient foe

Sails the Tyrrhenian sea to Italy.

Troy and her conquered Gods they with them
  bear.

Rouse then thy winds, whelm me the fleet in waves

Or drive disject, strewing the sea with dead.

Twice seven nymphs are mine, all passing fair,

But one above all fairest, Deïopeä:

Her will I make thy bride in wedlock sure,

With thee, for this high service, to abide

Thine own, and of fair issue make thee sire."

  To whom thus Aeolus: " Thy task it is,

O Queen, to well consider what thou wilt,

Nor sin for me thy hests to undertake.

Thou gainest me this realm, if realm it be,

Through thee I join the feast of Gods, through
  thee

The storm-rack and the tempest know me lord."

  He said, and turning, on the hollow hill

Smote with his spear : the Winds in serried troop

Rushed forth, and blew in hurricane through
    the world.
East wind and South together on the deep
Were fall'n, and ever-stormy Africus;
Up from the bottom torn they rolled the waves
Gigantic: noise of cries and cracking sheets
Mixed with their roar. Sunshine and vault of
    heaven
Forsook the Trojans' eyes; o'er all the deep
Darkness descending brooded. Pole to pole
Thundered, the dim air with quick-following flames
Flashed quivering; Death was there, Death nigh
    at hand.
   Aeneas shuddering groaned, and unto heaven
His hands up-stretching cried in agony:
"Ah happy, tenfold happy, ye who fell
Beneath Troy's walls, before your fathers' eyes!
Ah thou the Danaans' bravest, Tydeus' son,

Wherefore had I not died on Ilium's plain,

And yielded up my life beneath thy hand,

Beneath thy good arm yielding my last breath

There where Achilles' spear laid Hector low,

Where great Sarpedon lies, where Simois' wave

Shields, helms, and bones of warriors whirls

    along?"

  While yet he cried, a shrill blast of the North

Smote on the sail adverse, and higher still

Lashed the high waves: the oars beneath the

    strain

Snapped, the prow swerved, and left the ship's

    broad side

Bare to the breakers. Heaped on high to heaven

Came the huge mount of water towering on.

Some on the wave's top hang: some far below

Behold the bare earth mid the yawning sea

And mad surf boiling with the bottom sand.

Three ships the South wind caught and on hid
    rocks—

A monstrous ridgëd reef Italians call

The Altars—hurled them: three the East wind
    drave

Into the Syrtes' shallows on the lee—

Sight miserable!—and in the shoal entombed

Heaped them with sand. Another ship, that bare

Faithful Orontes and his Lycian crew,

Before Aeneas' eyes a whelming sea

Precipitate descending smote astern,

Headlong the steersman hurling; but the ship

Thrice in her place the violent eddy whirled,

Then all engulfed: within the monstrous pool

Swam scattered drowning men, and timbers torn,

And warriors' arms, and wasted wealth of Troy—

Now Ilioneus' good ship, Achates' now,

Abas', Aletes', the all-conquering storm

O'ercame; through starting seams their shattered
    hulls
Gaped miserably, and drank in the draught of
    death.
Meantime the roaring ruin of the main,
The storms unchained, the hid sea-deeps uptorn,
Neptune sore wroth perceived, and o'er the waves
Raised his calm head. He saw the Trojan fleet
Hurled all abroad and by the angry heavens
Ruinously rent; nor failed he to unveil
Juno's vindictive craft. He summoned straight
East wind and West, and thus upbraiding spake :
" What? Trust ye then so far your boasted birth?
Dare ye, unbidden of my sovran hest,
Raise this huge coil, and earth and heaven
    confound?
Ye winds whom I—but better boots it now
Still the vext seas. Another time offending

With other penalty ye rue the wrong.

Begone, and to your king this message bear:

To me, not him, was given by primal lot

The trident stern and empire of the sea.

The enormous rocks, O winds, your dwelling·

    place,

He holds his own: therein let Aeolus

Glory in his realm, and rule your prison barred."

    He spake, and lo, or e'er his speech was done,

He calmed the swollen seas, the gathered clouds

He chased away, and brought the sunlight back.

Cymothoë and Triton to the ships

Address them, and with strain from the jagged

    reef

Thrust off the keels: Neptune himself no less

Lifts them with succouring trident, carves their way

Through the huge quicksands, smooths the trou-

    bled waves,

And on light wheels o'er the calm ocean glides.

As when in some great throng hath strife arisen,

And through the savage mob runs sudden wrath,

Stones fly and brands—their frenzy serves them

    arms—

Yet if their eyes perchance some man espy

For duty and true service done revered,

They hold their peace, and stand with listening

    ears

Attentive; till his guiding words of peace

Soothe their hearts' storm: so all the outrageous

    sea

Fell silent, when the Father driving forth

Beneath the clear sky homeward wheeled his

    steeds,

And with loose rein sped on his flying car.

III.

THE FLIGHT FROM TROY.

(Virgil's *Aeneid* ii. 624–804.)

THEN saw I Ilium sink in gulfs of fire,

    And from her base uptorn Neptunian Troy.

As when on hills the vying husbandmen

Strive some old oak to o'erthrow, into his midst

Smit inly with redoubled strokes of steel:

With tremulous leaves the tree at every shock

Nods quivering; then, by iterated wounds

Quite vanquished, with one last life-uttering groan,

Along the rent hillside in ruin falls.

    I left the tower, and by convoy divine

Through flames, through foes I gat me; foemen's

    darts

Of me flew wide, and shrinking flames drew back.

But when to my old home I won my way,

And first my father to some mountain refuge

Fain would have borne, "Let me not live," he

    cried,

"To mourn in exile for our murdered Troy.

Nay, ye whose blood is yet of age undrained,

Your strength unworn, fly ye, and dare to live.

Had the Gods willed indeed my longer life,

My home they would have saved. Enough for me

One ruin to have seen, my Ilium's fall.

Let me lie here, and bid me one farewell.

Myself by my own act will find a death.

The foe may spoil, but yet will pity me:

A light loss is the losing of a tomb.

Too long already, all unloved of Heaven,

I drag my useless years, since these blind eyes

The Thunderer, Sire of Gods and King of men,

Scathed with the lighting's breath, and scared
  with fire."

He said, nor swerved : vainly with torrent tears

Myself, my wife, my child, and all his house,

Besought him that he merge not all in ruin,

And by his act drag down the impending death.

Still to his choice he kept, still clung to home.

Once more I sprang to arms—what else was left?

Once more in anguish prayed a warrior's death.

" Leave thee and fly ? Father, and hast thou
  deemed

Thus of thy son ? " I cried. " O impious thought !

If Heaven's hard sentence hath our race con-
  demned

To utter extirpation, none exempt,

If thy wild purpose hold, and thou must hurl

Thyself and thine to heap Troy's funeral pyre,

The way is plain, what hindrance ? Pyrrhus comes,

Drenched in the stream of butchered Priam's
    blood,
Pyrrhus, whose sword beside the altar's foot
Slaughters the son, and o'er the son the sire.
Was it for this, sweet Mother, thou didst lead me
Through foes, through flames—to see in this dear
    home
My sire, my wife, my child lie massacred?
To arms! their last day to the conquered calls.
Give me my battle back, give me the foe!
At least not unavenged this day we die."

   Thus yet again I girt me with my sword,
And in my shield resumed had thrust my arm,
And out of doors all desperate made my way,
When lo, my wife had flung her at my feet
Clasping my knees and stretching to my arms
Our child, Iulus. " If to certain death
Thou goest forth," she cried, "take us with thee!

But if not hopeless utterly, then stay,

Guard thine own home ! What shall befall thy
  child,

Thy father, and the wife once called thine own ? "

  So loud she wailed that all the dismal house

Rang to her cry; when lo, a sudden sign,

An omen and a miracle of heaven,

Smote us amazed. Before his parents' eyes,

Beneath their hands, on young Iulus' head

Blazed a light tongue of flame, and his soft hair

Crowned with innocuous light and bathed his brows.

Fain had our terror from that darling head

Dashed off the fire and quenched the holy sign.

More wise my sire refrained us; he to heaven

Raised his blind eyes and hands, and spake in
  joy :

  " Almighty Jove, if prayer may reach thine ear,

Look on us ; this sufficeth : if our souls

Prove duteous, grant thine aid, this sign confirm."

He said, and suddenly from the eastern heaven

Pealed thunder, and down-gliding through the

gloom,

Trailing his bright-lit brand, ran forth a star.

Far o'er the town the pilot meteor slid,

Track'd by his sulfurous furrow through the night,

And in the woods of Ida plunged his ray.

Then, then, my father yielded ; to the heavens

Again he turned, and called upon the gods,

And to that holy star did reverence.

"No more I tarry; where ye lead, I go.

Gods of our fathers, save us in this child.

Yours is this augury : in your ward is Troy.

Son, thou hast conquered; where thou wilt, lead

on."

Even as he ceased, more loud the on-rolling

fire

Roared, and the torrid blast breathed yet more

    nigh.

"Up, father, up," I cried; "my shoulders mount;

No pain to me such toil; whate'er befall,

Let both one peril find, one safety both.

Behind my footsteps follow wife and child.

Ye of my household mark; there is a mound

Outside the gateway, and a lonely fane

Built long ago to Ceres, thereanigh

A cypress, from old time a tree of awe;

Hither from diverse quarters tend we all.

Thy hand, my sire, must bear our sanctities,

Our household Gods ancestral, not to me

Permitted, in such sea of carnage stained,

Till I may cleanse me in the running stream."

    Thus saying I clothed on my shoulders broad

And my bowed neck with tawny lion-skin,

Lifting thereon my father; close behind

Creüsa followed, and with steps uneven
Our child, that wound his little hand in mine.
On through the dark we held. My heart, but
    now
By all the Danaän battle undismayed,
Sank, and at every gust, each trivial sound,
Trembled for them I led, for him I bore.
    And now I neared the gate, and deemed us
      safe,
When suddenly the tramp of thronging feet
Smote on my ear. "Fly, son," my father cried,
"They come. I catch the gleam of sword and
    shield."
Thereat I turned oblique and left the track—
Ay me! for some dark Power of will malign
Reft me of sense. Creüsa in that hour,
(O crowning woe of all that cruel night!)
Or wearied out, or wandering from the way,

Passed from our sight. Then only when we
    reached

The place appointed, Ceres' hallowed home,

I turned, I sought her; all the rest were there,

She only absent. Gods alike and men

Delirious I upbraided. Back I sped,

Leaving my comrades charge of sire and son,

Back to the flaming town. I drew my sword,

Ready once more for death, once more to range

Troy's wasted ways and join my doom with hers.

    First to the gate's dark threshold, crossed but
    now,

I gat me, and our footsteps backward. traced,

Shuddering; the very silence shook my heart.

Thence to our home. The Danaäns held it now,

To the roof's top rolled up the hungry flames

Exultant, wildly flaring to the wind.

Still on, to Priam's house, the heart of Troy,

I wandered.   There, in corridors forlorn

Of Juno's temple, watched beside their prey

Phoenix and fell Ulysses, guardians grim.

Here, pile on pile, Troy's treasure all around

Lay heaped at hazard – bowls of massy gold,

Rich robes, and festal tables of the Gods

Snatched from the burning shrines.   Children were

     there,

And women's quivering forms, war's living spoil.

I sought the streets, I filled them with my cries,

Reckless through deep despair, and called her name

With fruitless iteration o'er and o'er.

From door to door I raved, and found no rest;

When lo, the phantom form of her I sought,

Larger than human, rose before my eyes.

I saw, and stood amazed, and all my hair

Stiffened; my voice clave stifled to my throat.

The vision spake, my troubled soul was stilled:

"O my sweet husband, what wild grief is thine?

Not without God's will come these things to be.

That thou bear hence thy wife Fate's fixed decree

Forbids, and He who rules Olympus' realm.

Thee long exile awaits; wide waste of sea

Thy keels must plough; then shalt thou win a

    land

Far in the sunset, where thro' fertile fields

With kindly waters Lydian Tiber winds.

There all good hap, a realm and royal wife,

Are thine by lot. Weep not for me, thy love:

No haughty home of robber Myrmidons

Shall claim to hold in bonds, a captive slave,

Dardan Creüsa, wife of Venus' son.

Only the Gods' great Mother holds me here.

And now farewell, love thou thy child and mine."

She said, and while I wept and from full heart

Fain, fain had answered, faded into air.

Thrice strove I sore to fold her to my breast,

Thrice, clasped in vain, the phantom fled my arms,

Like the light wind or wings of flying sleep.

Meantime the long night waning wore away.

Back to my friends I fared, much wondering there

So great a host to find, Troy's remnant youth

For flight and exile gathered, piteous throng.

From all the conquered land they flowed and
    flocked

Ready with heart and hand to seek the shore

Unknown, where I might lead, beyond the sea.

And now the star of morning o'er the ridge

Of Ida rose, and led the springing day.

Around the gates of Troy the Danaän guards

Thronged vigilant; all hope of help was gone.

I rose, and raised my sire, and sought the hills.

IV.

THE ARMOUR OF AENEAS.

(Virgil's *Aeneid* viii. 608–731.)

NOW from on high amid the clouds of heaven
Venus descending came, and to her son,
Alone beyond the river far retired
In a deep glen, with welcome words drew nigh :
" Behold the promise by my craftsman lord
Accomplished; proud Laurentium to defy
And Turnus' strength thou with this gift, my son,
Misdoubt not": then, first clasped in his embrace,
Beneath an oak she laid the glittering arms.
He, glad at heart, o'er that high gift divine,
Unsatisfied with gazing, ran his eyes.
Much marvelled he, and handled o'er and o'er

The crested helm that shot terrific fires,

The fateful sword, the corslet mailed with bronze,

Blood-red and vast, as when a kindling cloud

Burns in the low sun's beam and flames afar.

The greaves he viewed, smooth work of gold refined,

The spear, and matchless miracle of the Shield.

Thereon had Mulciber, the Lord of fire,

Prescient of ages prophesied, inwrought

The destined triumphs of the race of Rome.

There lived Ascanius' line, and war on war.

First, the she-wolf within the cave of Mars

Couched, and the twin babes round her fostering teats

Played fearless; she her backward neck would bend

Fondling, and mould with lambent tongue their limbs.

Hard by, the lawless rape of Sabine maids

In open congress of the Roman games

Was figured, and the sudden war arose,

Tatius and his stern Cures matched with Rome.

Then, all their battle ended, lo, the kings

Erect in arms before Jove's altar stood,

Caught the swine's blood in cups, and sware a

    league.

Next these the hurrying cars asunder tare

Mettus—false Alban, thou hadst earned such

    doom.

At Tullus' hest his mangled limbs were borne

Wide through the wood, the brambles dripped

    with gore.

There too with mighty leaguer mustering round

Porsenna stood, and the free City bade

Take back the banished Tarquin, but her sons

In liberty's defence had leapt to arms.

I

Threatenings and wrath he breathed, for lo, the
  bridge

Behind Horatius whirled in ruin down.

Here Cloelia burst her bonds and swam the
  stream.

Here Manlius high on the Tarpeian hill,

Above the palace-thatch of Romulus,

Before the Capitol and shrine of Jove

Kept guard; along the golden colonnade

With silver wings the bird of warning flew,

Sounding alarm—the Gaul within the gate.

Amid the thicket swarmed the on-coming Gauls,

Safe in the darkness, the dim boon of Night.

Golden their flowing hair, their vesture gold.

Striped shone their cloaks; gold ringed their milky
  necks;

Long shields they bare, and brandished Alpine
  spears.

Here in their mystic dance the Salii moved,

And wild half-naked priests of Lupercal:

There were the flamen's fillets, there the shields

That fell from heaven: and in slow-rolling cars

Chaste matrons bare the sanctities of Rome.

Far hence were wrought the deep Plutonian realm,

And dread Tartarean torture of the damned.

Beneath a rock that threatened deadly fall

Hung Catiline; on the other side no less

The Furies' vengeful faces prest him hard.

Elsewhere, in bliss untroubled, dwelt apart

Souls of the just, and Cato gave them law.

Lastly, at large through all the shield there ran

The figured semblance of a swelling sea:

A golden sea with crests of silver foam,

And silver dolphins swam in circling chase.

Herein the bronze-beaked fleets, the Actian war,

Rode manifest; with ordered battle-line

Leucate glowed, and all the waves of gold.

Here, leading on the hosts of Italy—

Senate and People, Gods of Hearth and Heaven—

High on the deck the God-sent Caesar stood.

Round his glad temples trembled tongues of
    flame,

And o'er his head shone forth his father's star.

Elsewhere, with Heaven and Heaven's good wind
    to aid,

His armament Agrippa towering led;

Bright on his forehead gleamed his naval crown.

On the other side adverse, Antonius armed

Barbaric powers and warriors multiform,

Victor triumphant from the Red Sea shore

And the far lands of Morning: in his train

Rolled all the East from farthest Bactrian bound

To Egypt; ay, and Egypt's queen, his shame.

There clashed the enormous battle, there the sea,

Torn up with oars pulled home and plunging

    prows,

Foamed over all his face; almost it seemed

As though the unseated Cyclads, isle on isle,

Mountain on mountain hurled along the deep,

Shocked each with each, terrific tournament:

So huge the towered galleons teemed with men

Thronging, and from their hands flew iron darts

Or fiery; all the flood ran red with gore.

With native timbrels' clang the Egyptian queen

Roused in the midst her battle, nor beheld,

Nor yet beheld, behind her head the Asp.

Lo there the Dog Anubis and all forms

Of brutish Gods against Neptunus armed

And Venus and Minerva. Mavors there,

Graven in iron, raged, and in the air

Hung the dire Furies, and with riven robe,

Her symbol, Discord walked the murderous throng.

Behind, with bloody scourge, Bellona came.

Aloft, Apollo from his Actian shrine

Gazed over all, and bent his awful bow.

Thereat in terror all the Egyptian power,

Arabia, India, Saba, turned to flee.

Lo, here the queen herself invoked the winds,

Slacked all the sheets, and spread her flying sail.

Her mid the carnage, pale with coming death,

The Fireking fashioned, borne by wind and wave.

On the other side Nilus, a giant form,

Lamenting sore, opening his bosom wide,

Spread all his robe and called the conquered home

To his blue breast and shelter of his stream.

But through Rome's walls in triple triumph borne

Caesar to all the Gods of Italy

Three hundred shrines made holy evermore.

With glad applause and games the city rang.

In all the shrines a choir of matrons stood,

Altars in all, and slaughtered sacrifice.

Himself in Phoebus' glittering gate he sat,

Acknowledging the gifts of all the world.

Beneath, the vanquished hosts in long array,

Diverse in tongue and vesture, wound along.

Here Mulciber had moulded Nomad tribes

And Afric's loose-girt warriors, Leleges,

And Carians, and Geloni arrow-armed.

There moved Euphrates, now with milder waves,

And there the Morini, farthest folk of men;

Araxes' flood that never brooked a bridge,

And hornèd Rhine and tameless Dahae there.

All these on Vulcan's shield, his mother's gift,

Aeneas saw, and marvelled, what they meant

Unknowing; nathless on the imaged scenes

Well pleased he gazed, and to his shoulder hove

The fame and fortune of his sons to be.

ODE ON THE DEATH OF
GENERAL GORDON.

I.

ON through the Libyan sand
  Rolls ever, mile on mile,
League on long league, cleaving the rainless land,
Fed by no friendly wave, the immemorial Nile.

II.

Down through the cloudless air,
  Undimmed, from heaven's sheer height,
Bend their inscrutable gaze, austere and bare,
In long-proceeding pomp, the stars of Libyan
  night.

III.

Beneath the stars, beside the unpausing flood,

Earth trembles at the wandering lion's roar ;

Trembles again, when in blind thirst of blood

Sweep the wild tribes along the startled shore.

IV.

They sweep and surge and struggle, and are

     gone :

The mournful desert silence reigns again,

The immemorial River rolleth on,

The ordered stars gaze blank upon the plain.

V.

O awful Presence of the lonely Nile,

O awful Presence of the starry sky,

Lo, in this little while

Unto the mind's true-seeing inward eye

There hath arisen there

Another haunting Presence as sublime,

As great, as sternly fair ;

Yea, rather fairer far

Than stream, or sky, or star,

To live while star shall burn or river roll,

Unmarred by marring Time,

The crown of Being, a heroic soul.

VI.

Beyond the weltering tides of worldly change

He saw the invisible things,

The eternal Forms of Beauty and of Right ;

Wherewith well pleased his spirit wont to range,

Rapt with divine delight,

Richer than empires, royaler than kings.

VII.

Lover of children, lord of fiery fight,

Saviour of empires, servant of the poor,

Not in the sordid scales of earth, unsure,

Depraved, adulterate,

He measured small and great,

But by some righteous balance wrought in heaven,

To his pure hand by Powers empyreal given;

Therewith, by men unmoved, as God he judged

aright.

VIII.

As on the broad sweet-watered river tost

Falls some poor grain of salt,

And melts to naught, nor leaves embittering trace;

As in the o'er-arching vault

With unrepelled assault

A cloudy climbing vapour, lightly lost,

Vanisheth utterly in the starry space ;

So from our thought, when his enthroned estate

We inly contemplate,

All wrangling phantoms fade, and leave us face

    to face.

IX.

Dwell in us, sacred spirit, as in thee

Dwelt the eternal Love, the eternal Life,

Nor dwelt in only thee ; not thee alone

We honour reverently,

But in thee all who in some succouring strife,

By day or dark, world-witnessed or unknown,

Crushed by the crowd, or in late harvest hailed,

Warring thy war have triumphed, or have failed.

X.

Nay, but not only there

Broods thy great Presence, o'er the Libyan plain.

It haunts a kindlier clime, a dearer air,

The liberal air of England, thy loved home.

Thou through her sunlit clouds and flying rain

Breathe, and all winds that sweep her island

    shore —

Rough fields of riven foam,

Where in stern watch her guardian breakers roar.

Ay, throned with all her mighty memories,

Wherefrom her nobler sons their nurture draw,

With all of good or great

For aye incorporate

That rears her race to faith and generous shame,

To high-aspiring awe,

To hate implacable of thick-thronging lies,

To scorn of gold and gauds and clamorous fame ;

With all we guard most dear and most divine,

All records ranked with thine,

Here be thy home, brave soul, thy undecaying

    shrine.

March 1885.

WORKS BY ERNEST MYERS.

POEMS. Extra foolscap 8vo. 4s. 6d.

THE DEFENCE OF ROME, and other Poems. Extra foolscap 8vo. 5s.

THE PURITANS. A Poem. Extra foolscap 8vo. 2s. 6d.

THE EXTANT ODES OF PINDAR. Translated into English with an Introduction and short Notes. Second Edition. Crown 8vo. 5s.

MACMILLAN & CO., LONDON.

www.ingramcontent.com/pod-product-compliance
Lightning Source LLC
Chambersburg PA
CBHW020406030726
47496CB00007B/2336